Home in the Sky

Story and Pictures by
Jeannie Baker

Scholastic Inc.
New York   Toronto   London   Auckland   Sydney

ISBN 0-590-44704-1

Copyright © 1984 by Jeannie Baker.
All rights reserved. Published by Scholastic Inc., 730 Broadway, New York, NY 10003,
by arrangement with Greenwillow Books, a division of William Morrow & Company, Inc.
BLUE RIBBON is a registered trademark of Scholastic Inc.

12 11 10 9 8 7 6 5   3   6 7 8/9
Printed in the U.S.A.   09

Every day, at sunrise and sunset,
the pigeons burst into the sky.

The pigeons belong to Mike
and live on the roof
of an abandoned, burned-out building.
He built their coop from scrap lumber
found in the neighborhood.
Werewulf, Mike's dog, lives in the building
and guards the birds.

One morning, before feeding time,
Mike flies his pigeons as usual.

When Mike whistles, they know
it is time to come back for their food.
All the pigeons fly home,
except Light, who flies away.

After a while Light is very hungry.
He joins some street pigeons
who have found food.
But when Light tries to eat,
they screech, peck, and snatch
the food from him.

Light flies on....
It starts to rain.
His wings become heavy.

He flies through an open doorway.
The doors close behind him.
He is in a train.

A boy
picks him up,
holding him
firmly so he
will feel safe,
and gently
strokes his
feathers.

The boy walks home
cuddling Light to his chest.

He wants to keep the pigeon,
but his mother explains
that the band around Light's leg
means that he belongs to someone.

The boy places Light
on an outside windowsill
hoping he will stay.
But Light spreads his wings
and flies away.

Instinct tells Light
where to go.
He flies high over
unfamiliar buildings.

That evening,
as Mike is feeding his pigeons,
Light lands on his shoulder
and nestles against his face.

On his roof the next morning,
the boy eyes a flock of pigeons flying
in sweeping curves across the sky.
He is sure he sees a white pigeon among them.